Communities

Living Near a River

By Joanne Winne

Welcome Books

Children's Press
A Division of Grolier Publishing
New York / London / Hong Kong / Sydney
Danbury, Connecticut

Photo Credits: Cover © L. Kolvoord/The Image Works; pp. 5, 7, 9,11, 13, 15 © National
Geographic; p. 17 © L. Kolvoord/The Image Works; p.19 © Index Stock Imagery; p. 21©
Dammrich/The Image Works
Contributing Editor: Jennifer Ceaser
Book Design: Nelson Sa

Cataloging-in-Publication Data

Winne, Joanne
    Living near a river / by Joanne Winne.
      p. cm. — (Communities)
    Includes bibliographical references and index.
    Summary: This book discusses the lives of children who
live near various rivers in the world.
    ISBN 0-516-23302-5 (lib. bdg.) — ISBN 0-516-23502-8 (pbk.)
    1. Rivers—Juvenile literature 2. Stream ecology—
Juvenile literature [1. River life 2. Rivers] I. Title
II. Series
    GF63.W56 2000
    307—dc21

                                                                00-024037

Contents

My name is Abu (ah-**bu**).

I live near the Nile River in Egypt (ee-**jipt**).

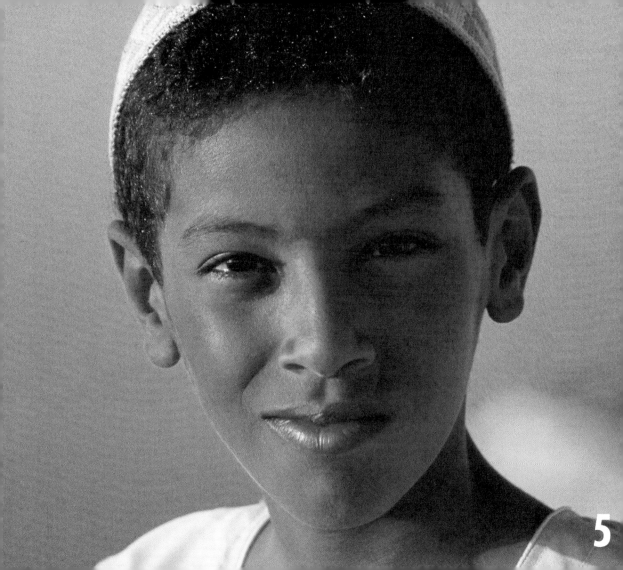

I live in a **village** along the river.

Many **palm trees** grow around my house.

My family has a **sailboat**.

I like to sail along the river.

The river is very quiet at **dusk**.

My name is Marco.

This is my pet parrot.

I live near the Amazon
(**am**-ah-zon) River in Brazil.

I live in a fishing village.

My father catches fish to sell at the market.

He ties up his boat to a **dock**.

13

I like to sit on my father's boat.

We take a ride down the river.

15

My name is Josh.

I live near the Colorado
River in Texas.

This is my **neighborhood**.

My house looks out over the river.

19

These are two of my friends.

They are trying to catch **minnows**.

There are many things to discover in the river.

New Words

dock (**dok**) place where people keep
their boats

dusk (**dusk**) the time just before it gets
dark

minnows (**min**-ohz) very small fish that
live in rivers and lakes

neighborhood (**nay**-ber-hud) the streets
and houses around where you live

palm trees (**pahlm treez**) tall trees with
no branches and many large leaves

sailboat (**sayl**-boht) a boat with a piece
of cloth called a sail; it moves by the
power of the wind

village (**vil**-ij) a group of houses, a small
town

To Find Out More

Books
Living Near a River
by Allan Fowler
Children's Press

The River
by Gallimard Jeunesse
Scholastic

Web Sites
Exploring the Vast Amazon
http://tqjunior.thinkquest.org
Discover the people, animals, and plants that live
along the Amazon. Then take the Amazon quiz!

Wild Egypt
http://touregypt.net/wildegypt/nile1.htm
Check out all the amazing sights along the Nile River.
Find out more about the cities, people, and animals
that use the river.

Index

About the Author

Joanne Winne taught fourth grade for nine years and currently writes and edits books for children. She lives in Hoboken, New Jersey.

Reading Consultants

Kris Flynn, Coordinator, Small School District Literacy, The San Diego County Office of Education

Shelly Forys, Certified Reading Recovery Specialist, W.J. Zahnow Elementary School, Waterloo, IL

Peggy McNamara, Professor, Bank Street College of Education, Reading and Literacy Program